THE COOLEST BEARD

Betty Tekle

illustrated by

Nicholas Alexander

Albert Whitman & Company
Chicago, Illinois

For Baba, who taught me kindness—BT

To Roberta Dunn, my loving grandmother
who was always supportive—NA

Library of Congress Cataloging-in-Publication data
is on file with the publisher.

Text copyright © 2023 by Betty Tekle
Illustrations copyright © 2023 by Albert Whitman & Company
Illustrations by Nicholas Alexander
First published in the United States of America
in 2023 by Albert Whitman & Company
ISBN 978-0-8075-1291-3 (hardcover)
ISBN 978-0-8075-1292-0 (ebook)

Printed in China

10 9 8 7 6 5 4 3 2 1 WKT 26 25 24 23 22

Design by Rick DeMonico

For more information about Albert Whitman & Company,
visit our website at www.albertwhitman.com.

This is my dad. And this is his beard. It's as long as the slide at the park and as thick as the bushes in our backyard.

Dad and I go to the barbershop every time we need haircuts and he needs a beard trim. Everyone always says hi to him. The guys at the barbershop crack jokes that make me laugh so hard my stomach hurts.

Sometimes they talk about other stuff that Dad calls "grown folks' business." I'm not allowed to listen.

I can tell they're talking about Mr. Williams though.

"Is Mr. Williams okay?" I ask Dad on our way out.

"Yes, he's okay. Nothing for you to worry about, Isaac."

"Dad, will I get a beard one day too?"
"Yes, son. When you're older," he replies.

"So, when I grow a beard, I can talk and listen to grown folks' business?"

Dad laughs. "Yes, son. By the time you get a beard, you'll be one of the grown folks."

I imagine all the things I could do with a beard.

Store snacks in it.

Use it to walk Peetie.

Jump rope with it.

I could even use it as a blanket.

But I don't want to wait.
I want a beard now!

The next week, when Dad has finished shaving, he rubs in drops of something I've never seen him use before.

"Dad, what's that?" I ask.

"It's called beard oil, kiddo," he replies. "It's the secret to how I keep my beard growing thick and healthy."

That's it! If I start using the beard oil today, by the time Dad needs another beard trim, I'll be getting one with him.

Week 1: Nothing yet.

Week 2: Still nothing. It's okay though.
I've got plenty of time.

Week 3: No need to panic, Isaac. Two more weeks till Dad's next trim.

Week 4: I see a hair! Oh, wait, that's just an eyelash. I know—I can use it to wish for an even longer beard.

Week 5: Argh! It's been over a month. Where is my beard?

Week 6: I just need a little more time. I already used up all of Dad's beard oil. I bet olive oil will work.

It's Saturday morning—barbershop day. I can't wait to show my beard to the guys. But when I run to the bathroom mirror, I see...nothing.
This can't be right.

My face is as soft and empty as the day before.
The beard oil really didn't work. There is no beard
blanket. No beard leash. No fun.

"You ready for the barbershop, Isaac?" asks Dad.

"I don't think I want to go," I say.

"What's wrong?"

The words spill out. "I'm sorry for using your oil without your permission, but I wanted to have a long beard, just like you, and be one of the grown folks."

Dad smiles at Mom then looks at me. "I think you should come to the barbershop. You might feel better."

"I don't know, Dad," I say.

"Come on. It'll be good," Dad says. He gives me a face-tickling beard hug until I agree to go.

When we walk in, Cliff says, "Hey, it's Dad's little mini-me. I hear you need a shave today."
"But I don't have a beard," I reply.
"Don't worry about that." Cliff winks at Dad.

I hop on Cliff's chair. He tells me to close my eyes until he's finished.

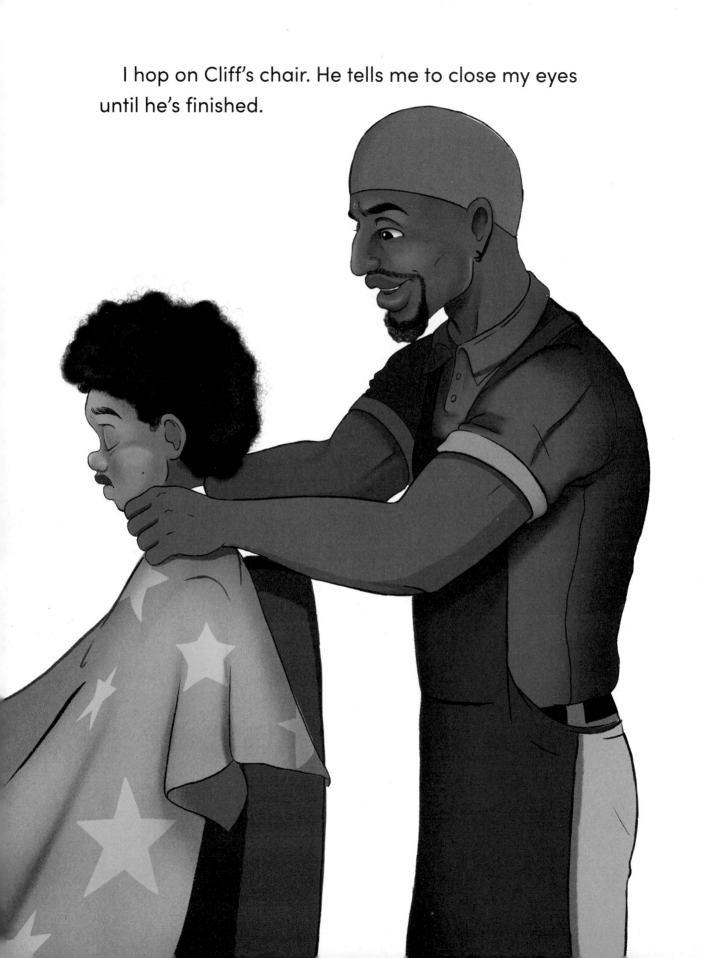

I feel something soft and fluffy on my cheeks, and I start to get excited. I wonder what it could be...

When I open my eyes and look in the mirror, I see that Cliff has put shaving cream all over my cheeks and chin. I look like Santa Claus!

My beard feels like a cloud. I have the longest beard in the room now.

"Look, Dad!" I exclaim.

"You look great, son," he says. "Actually, why don't you come here to talk with us, since you're one of the grown folks now?"

"I am?"

"You do have the coolest beard in the room."

I join the rest of the guys. We talk about Mr. Williams having a hard time getting around since he fell. Dad offers to run errands for him. Other guys also offer different kinds of help.

"Mr. Williams, I could walk your dog until your hip heals," I offer.

"Thank you, Isaac," he answers. I hear him say to Dad, "That boy is just like you, you know."

While Cliff wipes the shaving cream off my face with a hot towel, I see Dad give Mr. Williams something.

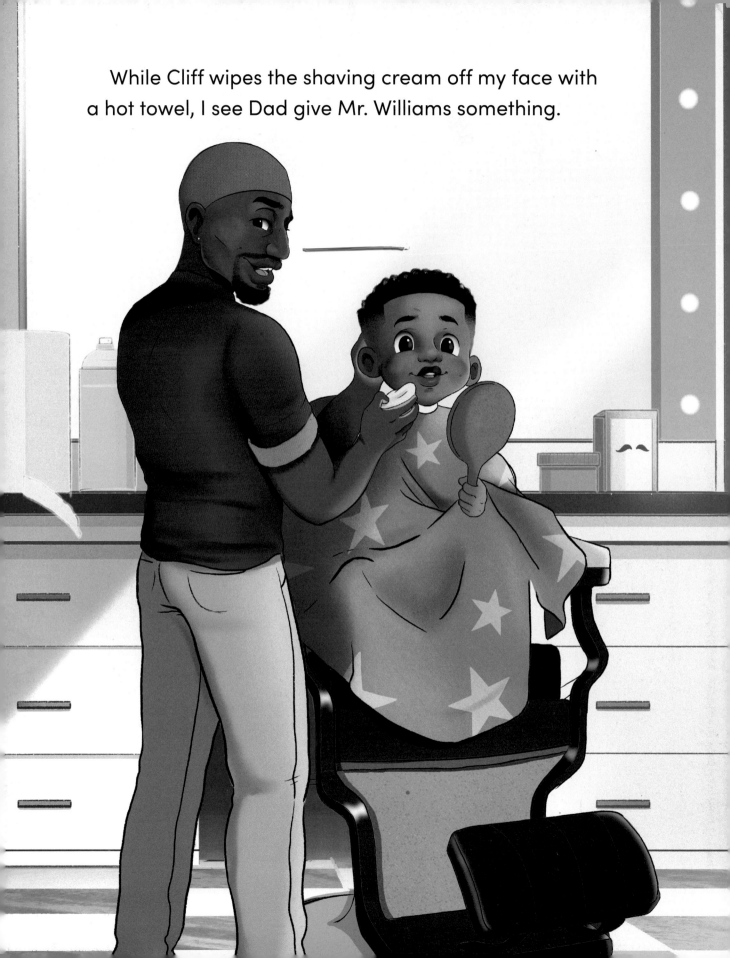

"Dad, why did you give Mr. Williams money?" I ask outside.

"He hasn't been able to work since he got hurt. I didn't want him to worry about paying bills," Dad says.

I didn't realize that grown folks' business is just adults helping each other.

Maybe it's not Dad's beard that makes him cool.

Maybe the coolest thing is the way he tries to take care of everyone. When I grow up, I'll take care of people just like Dad does.

Still, having a long beard would be cool too.